Copyright © 2003 by Harmen van Straaten
First published in Holland under the title *Het verhaal van Eend* by Leopold, Amsterdam
English translation copyright © 2007 by North-South Books Inc., New York

First published in the United States, Great Britain, Canada, Australia, and New Zealand in
2007 by North-South Books Inc., an imprint of NordSüd Verlag AG, Zürich, Switzerland.
Distributed in the United States by North-South Books Inc., New York.

Library of Congress Cataloging-in-Publication Data is available.
A CIP catalogue record for this book is available from The British Library.

ISBN-13: 978-0-7358-2133-0 / ISBN-10: 0-7358-2133-X (trade edition)
10 9 8 7 6 5 4 3 2 1

Printed in Belgium

Duck's Tale

by Harmen van Straaten

Translated by Marianne Martens

NORTHSOUTH BOOKS
New York / London

It was a hot and humid day.
Perfect for a swim, thought Duck.
I'm going to ask Toad if he wants to come along.

He walked over to Toad's house. Toad was sitting at his desk in front of the window. Duck heard him talking to himself.

"Ah hah," he said. "I see."

"Hello, Toad," said Duck. "Look what I found." Toad turned, looking up from his newspaper. He lifted up his reading glasses. "Oh," he said. "That's a pen—for writing."

"What are you doing?" asked Duck.
"I'm reading," said Toad, looking very important.

Toad had a big medal pinned to his chest. He told Duck that he'd gotten it for showing extraordinary courage. But according to Otter,

Toad had found the medal. Just like he had found the reading glasses.

"What are you reading?" asked Duck.

"Sorry. Very important stuff. Can't talk about it," said Toad seriously.

Duck was quiet for a while.
"Want to go for a swim?" he asked. But
Toad had bent over his newspaper again.

Duck dove into the water and swam to the bend
in the river where Otter and Hedgehog lived.
"Yoo hoo!" he called. But no one answered.

Slowly, Duck swam back to his house by the dock. Hmmmm, he thought. If Toad can read because he has glasses, then I must be able to write because I have a pen! I will write a story, and Toad can read it to me.

He sat on the dock, deep in thought, scribbling on some paper. From time to time, he'd close his eyes and concentrate, and then he'd start writing again.

"Hello, Duck!" someone called. Otter and
Hedgehog had come by in their boat.
"What are you doing?"
"I'm writing a story," said Duck.

"How clever," said Hedgehog. "I didn't know you could write."

"I didn't know either. This is my first try."

"Isn't it difficult?"

"Not at all. I'm just putting all my thoughts down on paper."

"When can we hear your story?" asked Otter.
"Tonight, when I'm finished," said Duck. "Please
come, and bring Toad. He'll need his reading glasses."

Duck wrote all day long. And when he was
finished, he looked at his reflection in the water,
and drew a self-portrait.
"I'm ready," he said at last.

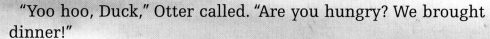

"Yoo hoo, Duck," Otter called. "Are you hungry? We brought dinner!"

After dinner it started to get dark. Duck lit an oil lamp.

"I'm stuffed," sighed Toad.

"Are you going to read us the story, Duck?" asked Otter.

Duck grabbed his papers and passed them to Toad. "Please, Toad? You have such a beautiful voice—and reading glasses!"

Toad looked at the papers with big eyes.
"Well, I don't know . . ."
"Please, Toad," said Otter. "You *can* read, can't you?"
Toad looked crossly at Otter. "I've been reading all day. My eyes are tired!"

"Please?" said Duck.
So Toad put on his reading glasses and took a deep breath. He looked at all the scratch marks and scribbles on the paper. "Hmmmmm," he said. And then he started . . .

"Duck's Tale"

"Once upon a time, there was a duck. He lived by the river, all by himself. Of course, he hadn't always lived alone. First he had lived with his mother and father.

"But one autumn, when it was cold and rainy, his parents flew south as most ducks do. 'Come with us,' they shouted. But he couldn't. His wings were still too small."

"How horrible!" shouted Hedgehog. "What happened next?"
Toad looked upset. "If you are going to interrupt me like that, then I'm going to stop reading."

He continued. "Winter came, and the river froze.
Duck couldn't dive for food anymore. He was very hungry
and sat shivering under a tree.

"Along came Otter. He brought Duck to his house, and together with Hedgehog, they warmed him up. Toad made a delicious soup. When winter was over, they built a beautiful house for Duck, and . . ." Toad hesitated, "they remained best of friends for ever and ever."

"What a wonderful story," whispered Otter.

"So exciting, too," said Hedgehog. "I wish I could write like you, Duck."

Duck looked at the ground. "Toad read it so beautifully," he said.

"Are you going to write another?" asked Hedgehog, just before they rowed away.

"Yes," said Duck. "If Toad will read it!"

Duck watched as the light from the boat grew
smaller and smaller. What good friends I have,
he thought. And happily, he went to bed.